C0-BEJ-373

Clock strikes five. Shop is closed.
Donuts sleep (so we suppose) . . .

—For Mimi, Tucker, and Steph.
May Judy's never close.

Copyright © 2018 by David Miles
All rights reserved.
Published by Familius LLC, www.familius.com
PO Box 1249 Reedley, Ca 93654.

Familius books are available at special discounts for bulk purchases, whether for
sales promotions or for family or corporate use. For more information, email
orders@familius.com.

Library of Congress Control Number
2017962461   pISBN 9781945547935   eISBN 9781641700283

10 9 8 7 6 5 4   First Edition   Printed in China
Illustration were created digitally.

BY DAVID MILES

DONUTS

THE HOLE STORY

Donut there.

Lots of donuts everywhere!

Some with frosting.  Some without.

Some with jelly in

Well *this* is a bit of a jam.

(and out).

Donut cops drive donut cars.

Donut trucks.

Donut trains.

Donuts trip to take a dip.

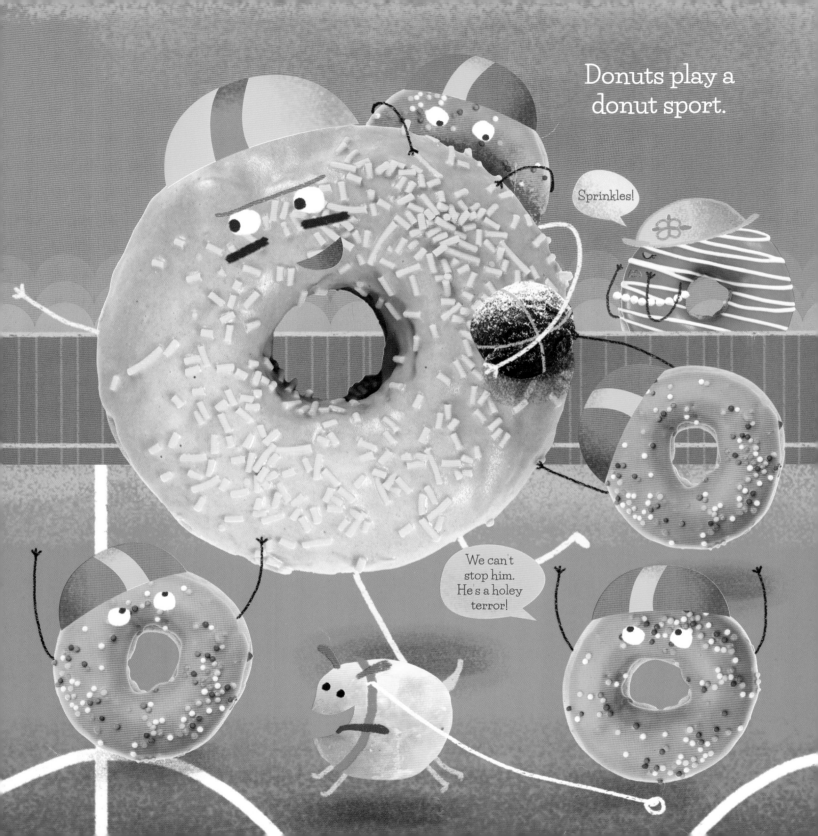

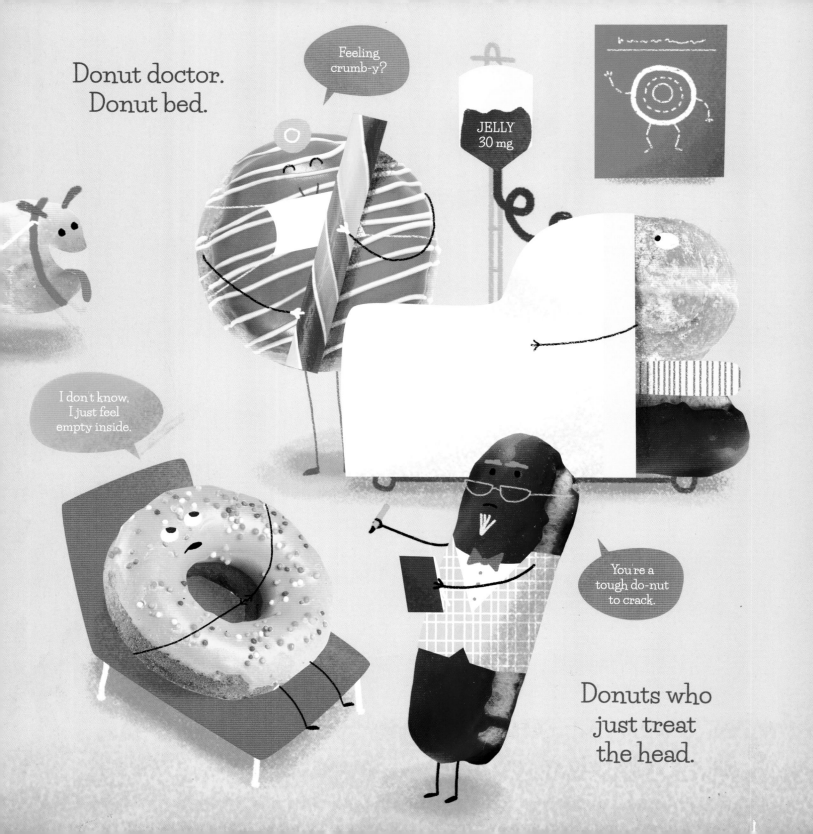

Donut farm where donuts grow.
Who is hiding in the row?

Robber runs.
Police car stalls!

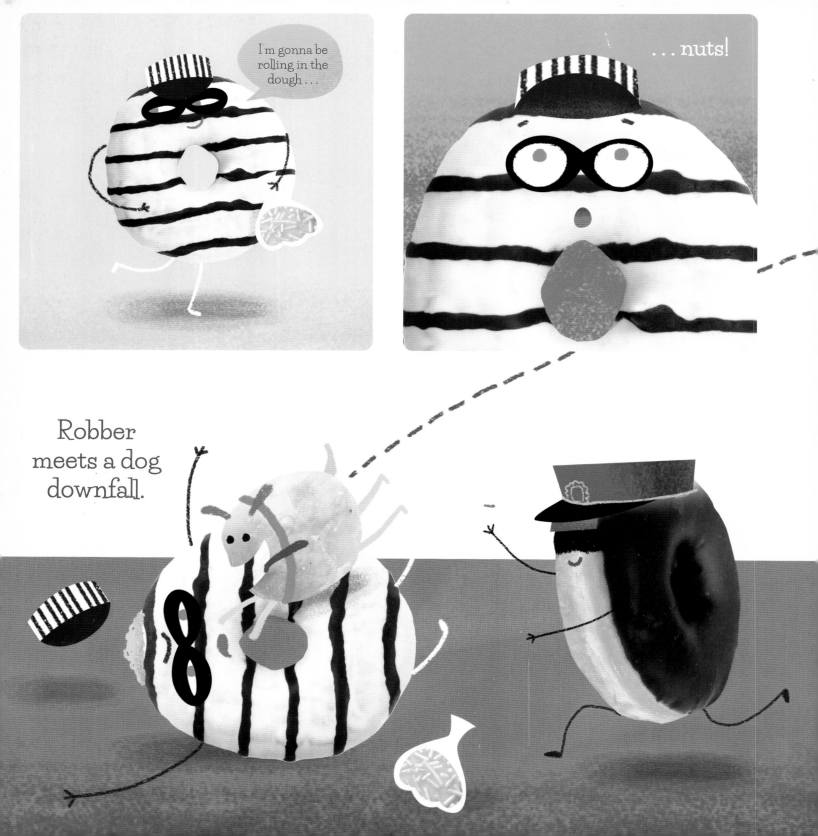

Morning nears, so donuts run. Donut night has been real fun.

Time to sprint and time to race
Back into the donut case.
Shoppers soon will want their treat.
Which one will they want to eat?

Donuts want a long lifespan.
Donuts craft a donut plan.
All must help: the cop, the crook,
Even Pan and Captain Hook.

Sun is up and rooster sings.
Shop is opened. Shop bell rings.
Time for donuts with the dawn, but

Only empty trays and bowls . . .

Donuts have a
knack for holes.